The Nurse Mare's Tale
By
Marta Moran Bishop
Cover Design - S.R Walker Designs

ISBN: 978-1-939484-56-7

When we first adopted Dinky from the rescue and learned about nurse mare foals, we were horrified. As we watched him grow into a beautiful horse, and I was writing Dinky: The Nurse Mare's Foal, I continued to think about not only these poor little foals and fillies who were forever motherless, but about the nurse mares and their loss. It was at this time I began The Nurse Mare's Foal.

It is entirely fiction, though has a basis in fact of how nurse mares are treated. Much like puppy mills, they are kept continually bred, and tossed away without thought when they can no longer give birth. The difference being that nurse mares do not get to nurse their own babies. They are bred for the sole purpose of coming into milk, for them to be rented out as nurse mares to milk the foal of a high dollar mare, so that that mare can be either bred again quicker or in shape to be shown again.

I did take poetic license to give this book a happier ending than nurse mares ever get.

I'd like to give a special thank you to Dinky, Chrome, and Connella who constantly give me delight and increase my knowledge of horses. Horses think, teach each other and remember more than we suspect. To my husband Ken Bishop, Sherrill Cannon, Karen Vaughan, and Robert W Walker who helped me immensely

Chapter One
Chapter Two
Chapter Three
Chapter Four
Chapter Five
Chapter Six
Chapter Seven
Chapter Eight
Chapter Nine
Chapter Ten
Chapter Eleven
Chapter Twelve
Chapter Thirteen
Chapter Fourteen
Chapter Fifteen
Chapter Sixteen
Chapter Seventeen
Chapter Eighteen
Chapter Nineteen
Chapter Twenty

ONE

This barn still has the scent of new wood, Sadie thought. Even though, I've been here nigh on eleven months it still smells new. It isn't like the old days, when all we had was a small field, without even a run in to get out of the sun or rain. This room is heaven, she thought. On the floor, the fresh cedar shavings nearly covered her hooves. There is more than just a dusting too. There is enough to have a roll in and to keep the smell of urine out of the stall. Of course, when I'm not breeding, I'm lucky to get shavings at all, but they want me to remain healthy, now that I'm so close to birthing. I wish they cared about my foal, she thought sadly. I know their only concern is for my milk so that I can feed another mare's foal.

"Ah there you are Nellie," Sadie said. "I have been thinking about the old days. Do you remember them?"

"I try not to think about them too much Sadie. So much of it makes me think of all the babies we lost. Sometimes, I do remember the fun we had when we were fillies before the breeding started."

"I know what you mean Nellie. Thinking about the old days makes me remember our babies too, or I think about the day we will go to auction. I'm so afraid that soon I will be too old, and they will put me on the block again. Or worse yet, the men will me put in the pen with the horses that they sell in a lot to some slaughterhouse in Mexico."

"Don't think of those things, Sadie. Try to focus on the good things. Like these beautiful rooms and how well we eat, when we are breeding or nursing."

"Didn't you have a filly a few years ago, Nellie? I had one about four years ago, and that year I got to nurse my baby. What heaven that was."

"Yes, I had one four years ago, and it was bliss spending those four months with it. I named her Sadie after you."

"You never told me that Nellie. It makes me happy to hear it. Did I tell you I named my filly Nellie after you?"

"Seriously? How wonderful." Nellie said shyly, her pleasure so deep that she couldn't put it into words, but Sadie knew she felt it

Restless, Sadie looked around. At the front of each stall, stood a double door, and between them, was a small room. "Nellie, I still laugh when I remember how hard we worked at trying to figure out what the small room was for, wasn't it funny? Of course, it does make it impossible for us to touch noses, but still we can visit over the divide."

At first, when the men brought them into these stalls, neither of them could figure out the purpose of the small space between the rooms. Until one day the Vet came, he put all his tools on the bench, hung his coat on the hook, and had a place to sit and discuss their health or write up his paperwork.

"Yes, that was funny Sadie, I still get a chuckle out of it too."

"Sadie, I'm going to go back outside for a bit. The air outside is beautiful today. There is a gentle breeze to cool me down. I'm sweating badly today. Perhaps it is the baby. I think it's because I'm getting closer to birthing. I wish they would let you go out too; the sun makes it is so warm for early April and the breeze is wonderful." Sadie watched her friend walk out of the door in the back of her stall, into the small paddock behind it. *I wish I could go out today too,* she thought. *It would be nice to feel the warm sun on my mane and smell the air. I'm so restless today; it would be pleasant if the paddocks were large enough to get up a decent run.*

The snow has melted, and most of the dirt is dry. I could watch what is going on in the rest of the farm. That would be fun, at least it would take my mind off what's to come. She thought, looking out of the door onto her paddock.

In the dry seasons, the earth in her paddock was dusty, and it was muddy in the wet seasons. It had a single tree off to one side of it, on the other side of the fence. Sadie wished the tree was close enough that she could chew the bark, thus cleaning, and filing her teeth, but at least it gave her shelter from the sun, and rain. During the day, she spent most of her time out in the paddock; it was during that time that the workers cleaned the stalls. *The place had sure changed from the days when I was young,* she thought.

I wish Nellie, and I could share a paddock. It would be nice to feel like we were a herd. It is not natural for horses to be alone, and very strange to have to go into the stall to visit. At least I can view the other horses that live in the barns near mine, and if the wind is blowing just right, we can talk a bit.

I can watch the comings, and goings of the men and women around the farm. That is always amusing. And I can watch the clouds move across the sky; and the birds fly. It makes me sad to watch the horses in the far-off fields. Sometimes I pretend to be a part of the herd, though I know I'm not and never will be. I'm overthinking today; I wish Nellie would come back in so we could talk.

TWO

While she waited, she eyed the lone cobweb that clung to the rafters, watching the spider climb across the web wondering how someone had missed it. It was not typical for them to leave a cobweb in the stalls; she had heard the cleaners say webs caused fires. She continued looking around her room; *I want to remember everything.* On one wall hung her water bucket and feed dish. In the corner lay a pile of hay, enough for a breeding mare. *Why are my foals unimportant?* she thought, as Nellie came back in. *It's kind of her to give up her time in the sun to keep me company.*

"Nellie, your baby is coming late isn't it?"

Nellie's brown coat and golden mane are so beautiful; I wish I'd stayed black or had a golden mane too. We have been friends for so long, ever since we met at the auction, before they brought us here twenty-two years ago. I wish I looked like Nellie. Maybe, if I weren't white, the men wouldn't call me Ghost. I hate that name; it makes me feel invisible.

"I think so Sadie, and it worries me a bit. The men took me out three times this year to the breeding field."

"Nellie, what will happen to you if the baby comes too late for you to milk another's foal?"

"I try not to think about that Sadie. They won't want me around here just eating and taking up space on the off chance that next spring I'll breed again and can milk another mare's foal. Not at my age, they won't keep me around. My breeding days are over Sadie and they have a large crop of new fillies ready for breeding, so they wouldn't want my baby even if it's a girl."

"So are mine, Nellie. I want so badly to keep this baby. I fear for it, for you, your baby, and for me too. I think this is the last day that I will see you Nellie, at least at this farm. We must talk and see if we can't figure out a way for you to at least keep your baby; that is, if it is born too late."

"I know you are right. But I hate the thought of thinking about it all, let alone talking about it. You've always been the planner Sadie. I've been the go alonger."

"You are my best friend Nellie. We aren't that old, even if our breeding days are over. I don't want to lose you, and I don't want us to be taken to auction. We both know what happens to mares our age at auction. Nellie, our time together is running out. My baby will be here tonight or tomorrow. The men will come to take me away soon."

"Oh Sadie, tonight?"

"Yes! But perhaps we can have a few bright moments of talk today too."

"Please, I think I can bear the dark talk if we have a few happy moments too."

"Did you see the fillies in the little field, Nellie? Running, jumping, and having so much fun."

"Yes, Sadie. I even saw my little one. She is more beautiful than the first day. Which one is yours?"

"The little black one with the blaze on its forehead." It will be four soon."

"So, will mine, Sadie. The humans will separate them from the younger ones and put the 'stallion' in with them soon."

"You are right, but let's not think about that today; but instead think about the sweetness of them and the wonder of spending those four months we had with them."

"Agreed."

"We were lucky Sadie; our fillies came at the right time for the men or we wouldn't ever have had the chance to nurse our own."

"Right you are Nellie most nurse mares never get to nurse their own and it doesn't seem to matter if it is a foal or a filly. If the men hadn't known they'd need more nurse mares soon when we had ours, they would have been ripped from us just as the foals are, and we'd have been sent to nurse the Elite foals that season too."

"How sad that would have been Sadie."

The sweet smell of freshly cut hay filled the air; it was ecstasy. It is too early in the year for haying.

"Nellie did a new shipment of hay arrive today? You can see from your side of the farm when you are out in your paddock."

"I'll go look, Sadie. I haven't been paying attention today; it will just take a minute. I'll be right back." Nellie sauntered out of her stall, with an air of relief from a break in the dark musings of her friend.

I wonder if they know that it is almost time for the birthing? I've eaten little. I'm bored and cranky, she thought, shifting positions again. It is a beautiful day for early April; seldom was the weather this grand so early in the year this far north. It wouldn't hold, but it was so pleasant to see something other than the white of snow and the gray sky. It would have been delightful to take a nap in the sun today. Soon it will be suppertime.

"The new hay came today," Nellie said perkily.

"You should eat well tonight my friend. I doubt I will be here for it. They will probably move me to the birthing field tonight."

THREE

Thank the gods that Nellie could come and go from her paddock to her stall and has spent so much time inside today. She is taking pity on my loneliness. She had always been sweet to me, Sadie thought, reminiscing about the days when they had been fillies together, those were fun days. Before, we knew what life had in store for us! Shaking herself out of her thoughts, she said.

"I probably will never see this room again. I don't like to think about why, Nellie. I do know; they will take my baby away after I give birth. With no time to mourn the loss. The men will trailer me from the birthing field to the fancy barn. There, I will nurse the other foal, and they will treat me like a queen for a few weeks. My every desire met, if it will make the foal happier and healthier. It's after the weaning that I'm afraid of Nellie.

I think the men will feel that I am too old to be bred again. I am frightened of what will happen next, and I am afraid of what will happen to you and your baby too."

"Sadie!!" Was all Nellie could answer.

"I want to remember this room, and this year with you. I've been happier now than I've been in an extremely long time."

"Me too Sadie. The last time I was this happy was when I nursed my filly, and when we were just little fillies ourselves."

Sadie looked out the top of the double door at the end, of the stall; she could see many other barns like this one. If I look past all the small paddocks, way off in the distance, I can see the grassy fields sectioned off by fencing. Groups of horses roamed in the sunlight, eating a bit here and a bit there. They look almost like a herd, yet there are no foals to make it so, she thought.

Past those fields lay the far fields, the mares birthing fields, they would come for her soon and take her to one of them. "Did I ever tell you what happened to my first baby Nellie?"

"No Sadie, do you need to talk about it today?"

"If you wouldn't mind Nellie. It is weighing on my mind.

I've been praying they won't take me to the field where I gave birth to my first baby. It is the field that is the farthest out. A wolf pack came right after I gave birth and tore my baby apart. There wasn't anything I could do. I just laid there too weak and watched those wolves ripping my first foal apart, gnawing on its little body. There were too many of them and exhausted from labor; I couldn't stop them. It would have been me next, but the men showed up. Oh God Nellie, they acted as if the wolves had done them a favor."

"Are you afraid it will happen again, Sadie?"

"I've been watching; the other fields are full of mares that will be birthing soon. I'm afraid they will bring me to that field, Nellie. It still frightens me; it's as if the ghosts of the past will catch up to me with my last baby."

"Oh, dear friend that is the most horrible story I have ever heard. How did you keep going after that Sadie? Are you afraid every time you are going to give birth, that it will happen again? I think I would be."

"Yes, a bit of me is afraid each time, but not as afraid as I am this year. Why don't you go out in the sun for a spell Nellie? I'll clear my mind, and we will plan something, and maybe we can protect us all."

"Sadie, I wish I could have your food if you aren't going to eat it.' Nellie stated wistfully, walking in again from a stint in her paddock. 'You have been short-tempered all day; it probably does mean the baby is coming tonight?"

"Nellie. I hear the diesel engine now. It could be the men would you go outside and look for me?" As Nellie turned to go, Sadie said, "Nellie, you know I won't be back. If they send us both to auction, we must find each other in the crowd of horses; I will have a plan then. Just find me okay?"

"I will Sadie. Remember I love you, and always have." Nellie said walking out of her stall.

FOUR

"Why do you call her the Ghost?" Tom asked Sam, as they sat in the cab of the truck.

"She is almost white now and has been extraordinarily meek and mild-mannered since her second foal. One hardly remembers she is there most of the time." He replied.

There was a sly lazy air about Tom. He was a bit slovenly, his long hair hanging greasy on his shoulders, a few strands combed across his prematurely balding head. Sam could hardly bear the smell of him; a combination of oily hair, and a pungent smell of stale beer clinging to him.

"Will you open the window a bit, Tom?" Sam asked. He wears his blue jeans in what humans commonly referred to as a plumber's crack; I don't see how he can walk properly. I will have to get the boss to discuss his clothes. It won't do, working with horses.

The red truck backed up to the gate of Sadie's paddock. "Tom would you please go open the gate for me?" Sam asked.

"I'll take a look-see, Sadie and be right back," Nellie said as she walked back out to her paddock. Poking her head back in Nellie said, "One of them is old Samuel, but the shorter man looks like a real greenhorn, Sadie. I never saw him before. He is a little man, a bit sly looking, with a mean look in his eye, and the smell of cruelty." Both mares' ears perked up to hear the two men outside the small barn.

"Tom here's the rope, go get the Ghost. You can bring her out through the paddock. I'll be waiting at the trailer for you. She will be a bit cranky, but education is what you are here for. Besides I am here to train you, not to do the work."

"Sam, which one of them is the Ghost, and if she is cranky, what's the best way to get the rope around her?" Tom asked cunningly.

"How long have you been around horses Tom? Surely long enough to know what a freaking halter is. Just go up to her, whisper sweet things to her, and put the lead rope on the ring. It is the ring on the chin strap at the base of the halter." Sam shook his head in disgust. *What the hell did the boss think when he sent this useless piece of shit to him for training? I bet Tom can't even tell the difference between a forelock, and a frog. Maybe the guy was just lazy, though he might be like some people who acted stupid so they can get out of doing chores,* Sam thought.

"I hear Nurse Mares have become a big business?" Tom said, to delay going into the barn. His voice full of bravado, but the mares could smell his nerves even with the barn doors closed. They could hear it in his voice. It worried them. As they waited, Sadie paced.

Fear is not an admirable trait in men. In some men, it brought out a real mean streak, in others just cowardliness. It is then that horses and men get hurt. She heard the craftiness in his voice, and that nasty streak Nellie talked about.

"Oh, give me the stupid rope; we'll be here all day if we continue this way. Now move out of my way, and watch. Next time it will be your turn." Sam said in frustration.

Sadly, Sadie looked at her friend Nellie. "There is no time left Nellie. Remember to look for me if we must go to auction. I hope we see each other again. I shall miss you." She wished they could touch noses for the last time, but the small room between the stalls did not leave the possibility of getting close. She backed up into the corner of the room. Her eyes looked around the room with longing, sniffing its smells, filling her heart with a last glance. Hopefully, it would be enough to last a lifetime in her memories. She hoped they would bring her back to this room after she had weaned the new foal but doubted it. It had never happened before, so she did not believe it would happen this time. I am so tired of losing everyone. I know they rarely let any of the mares become too comfortable together. Still, she hoped that this time would be different.

I am so afraid that I will never see Nellie or the other mares again. I am frightened, Sadie thought as the door opened, and Samuel walked in, rope in hand.

FIVE

Nervously, Sadie waited; Samuel's usually calm voice had a hint of anger in it tonight. *Why is he mad at me?* she thought nervously. With a last glance, at her friend, to say goodbye, and wishing again that they could at least touch noses, she waited. With the rope already clipped on her halter, she felt cornered. She had never felt like this around Samuel before, but then she had never felt his irritation before.

As he led her out of her stall into the paddock, she saw the trailer and the little man standing next to it. She did not like his look. He walked with a swagger, his legs barely bending at the knee. He reminded her of someone she saw at the auction years before when she was a young filly. The look in Tom's eyes was one of crazed glee. It seemed out of place considering his fear, and he smelled dirty. He frightened her more than she wanted to admit.

There's no point in fighting, she thought, I must keep up my strength. Struggling will not change the outcome, and only makes everything more complicated.

I am already lonely; Nellie was the best friend I ever had. They had been friends from the time they were fillies. Even though they had not seen each other in years, when their eyes met it was as if they had never been apart. It may be the last time we see each other, she thought sadly, as Samuel led her up the ramp into the trailer.

She knew the trailer meant they would take her to the far field. That first field, the one where she had her first baby., Panicking at the idea of going there, she balked before entering the trailer. I do not want to go to that field, please she begged. Out of the back of his jeans, Tom pulled a short crop, called a bat and hit her. He was behind her to her right, and with her on the ramp, she could not fight. Tom hit Sadie harder than she had ever experienced it before, and he did not stop, but continued to beat her with the crop, all the while he yelled, "Get up the ramp bitch." Samuel screamed at him, louder than she had ever heard him yell before. Samuel yelling added to her fear, and she reared. Fearful of falling on the ramp. She backed up, right into Tom, jumped from the ramp, and ran. For one single moment, Sadie felt free. It was all an illusion and she was trapped and with nowhere to go.

Her coat drenched with sweat she shivered in terror. She stood with her back against the fence. Even Samuel could not get close to her with his soft voice and a gentle hand, so frightened was she.

"What in the freaking hell were you doing? And what are you doing with that bat?' He yelled at Tom. 'Get out of here! Do not turn around, and do not bother to stop at the house. Whatever you have coming to you, for the few hours you have been here, we will mail to you. Though, the lord only knows why you deserve even that."

"I don't know who in the hell you think you are Sam, but I will talk to the boss, and we will see if I leave or not." Tom said stomping off.

Sam continued standing just inside the paddock, murmuring to Sadie, "Shush girl, good Ghost, everything will be okay now. He will not be back to hurt you girl." Crooning at her, Sadie only watched him, ears back. *She had never been beaten before or at least not since that time the men took her baby away, that first time. I was so young then, and still believed I could fight these men. But it was such a long time ago. She had fifteen babies since then. Now she knew differently; the men acted as if they were her gods*

21

and not her keepers. She was the prey, and they were the predators. They owned her and were her masters, even those that were evil like Tom.

Samuel walked out the small gate, and away from the paddock. She heard him dialing on the small device he pulled from his pocket. She couldn't hear anything from where she was. Soon he was talking excitedly to someone. Sadie had seen the men use these things before; she knew it always meant someone else showed up. She didn't understand, and how it worked but knew it was a way of communicating with others. *Soon someone else will be here; someone always showed up.* At least it will not be Tom she thought, and hoped he never came back.

Sam had left her alone to calm down but was still just outside her corral. She eyed him nervously, soon he walked over, and began crooning kind words to her again. "You're a good girl Ghost; it is okay girl." Sadie wanted to scream, *my name is not Ghost, but knew that wouldn't do any good either, and wondered why Samuel always called her Ghost? Doesn't he know that calling someone names did not exactly endear you to them?* Still, he went on quietly, soothingly. "Shush girl, it will be fine now, he is not coming back," Over, and over Samuel said these words, and she began to quiet.

Nervous, and ready to run at the least thing, the rope still hanging from her halter, Sadie feared to move. If she walked in the wrong direction, the rope would hit her on the side of her neck or worse it could get under her feet and trap her. Sam continued to sing, the edge gone from his voice, but he didn't try to touch her.

Out of the corner of her eye, she saw the boss coming. He looked furious, not containing his anger he began yelling at Sam. "Who do you think you are firing my new man? What made you think you had the right, Sam? I'll have you know he is my brother's son, and he will be back tomorrow. My brother asked me to take him on for a spell, keep an eye on him, and teach him a bit. I'll have no more of your shenanigans, Sam. He told me that you were in a foul mood, and took it out on him, and the mare. You have been here long enough to know how I feel about mistreating the animals, Sam. What is wrong with you anyway?"

Sadie listened nervously to the boss. *I've never heard him go on so long, nor have I heard him treating Sam like this before.* It made her even more hyper, and warier. Belly heavy with her kicking foal, it was warm for early April, wet as she was from sweat, the brisk breeze made her shiver. She wished everyone would go away and leave her alone. She knew she stunk of fear and wanted to dry off and feel the clean air on her hide again.

Quietly Sam said. "I do not know what that fool told you Mr. Bentley, but he beat the mare pretty badly when she bulked at going into the trailer. Look at her all lathered up over there. I did not even know he had a bat on him. In the thirty odd years I have been with you, have you ever seen me hit any animal? You have always been a fair man, Mr. Bentley, and one that knows the truth when he hears it."

"I believe you, Sam,' Mr. Bentley said quietly. 'I am not sure what I am going to do about young Tom, I don't like him, but I promised my brother. That will be a problem for a different day, though if he is an animal abuser, I do not know what I will do."

Shaking hands, the two men, looked at Sadie. "Let's get the mare calmed and loaded."

SIX

Walking over to her paddock, the two men stood quietly, at the fence, and just watched her. Now and then they'd look at each other. Inspecting the two men warily, Sadie waited. Walking through the gate into the enclosure Sam began his crooning again. "Good Ghost, easy girl, all is fine, and all will be well." His hand lightly picked up the rope as he came closer a little hum in his voice interspaced with a good girl, easy Ghost. He began rubbing her down first with his hand. Still crooning, the boss handed him a soft towel, soon he was rubbing the sweat off her body with the cloth, while he hummed.

Finally, calmed, and dry again, he took the rope, and slowly led her back out of the gate toward the trailer. Still, Sadie balked, but this time the two men were ready, with a gentle hand Sam petted, and soothed her, all the while leading her up the ramp. Meanwhile, the boss with his hand on her backside gently pushed her up the slope into the trailer. Sam leading, and Mr. Bentley taking the back, Sadie was finally in the trailer and the ties in place. She could reach the hay manger if she did want to eat. It was not to be a long trip. It was just too long of a walk for the men. With her heavy with foal, both men knew it was a terrible idea to ride her so close to birthing. Her work had stopped about two months earlier, the most exercise she had was the movement of walking in her paddock. So trailering was the way to go.

With all the other fields full, the decision had been made to put her in the backfield. They hadn't used that field since the episode with the wolves some twenty odd years ago, but the wolves had left the area, and the men believed it safe now. Neither of them would have thought she remembered the field, or that is what frightened her.

Tied up firmly in the trailer, uncomfortable, sweating, and frightened Sadie let out a loud, sharp squeal that seemed to go on, and on. Looking at each other the two men tried to understand why the Ghost had suddenly become so verbal; she was not her usual docile self at all. The mare barely made a whisper or groaned that anyone had heard in years. She was nearly white with age now, and had been silent, and meek since the first foal twenty-two years ago. In fact, she was such a quiet mare; they began calling her the Ghost. No one noticed or paid attention to her as she wandered around. In fact, no one had in many a year. Oh, they would feed her, house her, and breed her, but not notice her, she was not real. She appeared broken without personality or spirit. Quietly she nursed each new foal, and then bred again, the cycle continued year after year.

Now the very air quivered with her screams. Samuel went in the trailer, and checked all her vital signs, checked the heartbeat of the foal. The Ghost, and the foal were in excellent condition, even the whip marks that Tom had laid on her barely showed. She still screamed whenever they shut the doors.

Sam stood there with her petting, and rubbing Sadie, crooning, and singing to her. Turning to Mr. Bentley he said, "boss, can you bring Nellie? I think that is the only way we will keep her quiet, and make sure she doesn't hurt herself. We have Star's foal due shortly and have no other mare to nurse it."

"Not to worry girl, you aren't going to travel alone. Nellie's coming girl; you'll be together now. You won't be alone girl." he whispered to her repeatedly until they could both hear the boss on the ramp with Nellie. Soon both mares were tied in tightly, and the doors closed to the trailer. All was well, the screaming had stopped.

"What will we do with Nellie, Sam? How will we manage to separate them?"

Walking away from the trailer, out of hearing of both horses, Sam said. "Truth is I sometimes think the horses understand us. Now here is the plan. When we get to the field, pull the back of the trailer only far enough into the field so we can close the gates at the back of it, leaving nothing else out. Then I'll walk the Ghost out, behind me start to bring Nellie, but go slowly; you need to stay close enough you can tie her up again without the need to move her back into the trailer. After I get Sadie in the run-in, tie Nellie back up, and shut the doors of the trailer, move it out, and close the gates."

"Do you think it will work Sam?"

"Only if you move the trailer far enough down the road that it is out of sight of the field. Even in her condition, I am afraid she would try something. I'll cut through the fields and walk the five miles back. You keep going, okay? Tomorrow when we bring her some hay, she will be fine. Whatever is bothering her will be forgotten I'm sure."

"Sounds like a good plan Sam. Any idea what is wrong with her?"

"I wish I could tell you, Mr. Bentley. I genuinely have no idea what's the matter with the Ghost today, she has never been like this before. I wish we could get this over with soon, but I daren't drive faster over these bumpy roads. We could break an axle or hurt her. Luckily it is not far, but we do have to take it slowly. It's too bad all the other fields are full, and we have so many mares birthing this year that we must use that field."

"I know Sam; it isn't your fault that the only field open this spring is the backfield. She'll be okay when she gets back there. It has a nice little run in now, so she will have protection from the elements. "She only has to stay out there till Star has her foal. We can sure use the money that these nurse mares bring. Losing two mares this winter sure dug into the profits, then with the cost of feed, and fuel, well you know what I mean Sam. This year's nurse mare crop should make up for that though." Mr. Bentley yelled over the noise of the diesel engine.

Then both men fell silent, trying to block out the sound of anguish, utter fear, and loneliness coming from the trailer. They found it odd that even with Nellie for company, still, the Ghost whimpered. At least the screaming had stopped. Luckily the drive finally ended, the truck stopped.

"Let's get this show on the road boss," Sam said, opening the back of the trailer. Sadie stood there tied, looked mournfully at him; he could swear she was crying. Nellie nuzzled her as best she could, but it only seemed to console her a little.

Mr. Bentley looked at Sadie; her eyes peered at him with such anguish he wanted to cry himself. Now get a grip on yourself man, he thought. Whatever will Sam think of your imagination, not to mention your desire to cry? Whatever is wrong with us all today? he thought.

Slowly whispering, Sam started down the ramp out of the trailer; put a rope on her halter after giving her a bit of a rub down. Mr. Bentley was standing next to Nellie. *Good thing this was one of the big trailers,* he thought, *or we wouldn't both be able to get in with the two horses.*

"See you on the other side boss," Sam stated as he led Sadie down the ramp and out into the field. Her entire body was shaking as he walked her over to the run-in. "Don't worry girl; all will be okay." He crooned. Once in the run-in, unable to see the truck any longer, Sam began brushing her, talking and singing to her, calming her as best he could. Suddenly the sound of the truck engine started. Sadie jumped, tried to rip the rope from his hands, and run out of the shelter. Holding on for dear life, happy he had also thought to tie it to the post, Sam continued to talk to her. Soon they heard the gate closing, and the truck moving off.

SEVEN

Sadie looked at Sam in disbelief. He had lied to her, tricked her. She had never known him to do such a thing. Her shaking began again, and she pulled at the rope harder and harder.

As soon as they could no longer hear the truck, Sam untied her, and began to rub her down again, walked her around the field, let her look at the woods and inspect the place to her heart's content. Slowly, calming down, she found a little patch of clover, the pile of hay, and water in the trough that they left for her. When she finally appeared calm, Sam undid the rope, walked a bit away from her, and sat down on a rock. Keeping an eye on her to make sure she was okay before he left her to begin his trek back to the barn.

"Ghost, soon it will be dusk girl, I must be making my way back to the barn. I still have other chores to do, and it is a hike even through the fields." Sam told the horse, walking to the fence, and climbing over. Taking one last look at her began his walk.

"Sure, hope the boss sends someone up to meet me somewhere along the line. If not, I won't be back before dark.' He said talking to himself.

'What a day. I can't believe the Ghost remembers that field after twenty-two years. I know it is where her first foal died by the teeth of the wolf pack, but it is impossible that she remembers. She is just a dumb animal, and not even as smart as some of the other horses. She's a nurse mare for god's sake,' He told himself again as his long stride covered the acres walking across the fields of hay growing in the deepening afternoon's sun. 'Wish I had remembered to have him leave a water bottle behind. I'm sure thirsty." Just as he said that to himself, he heard the faint sound of an engine coming toward him. *Thank god, the boss sent someone for me,* was his last thought before he saw the truck coming over the rise.

"Howdy Sam, long time no see," joked Mr. Bentley, handing him a bottle of water. "Expect you are thirsty?"

"Didn't expect you to come, boss, I sure hoped you'd send someone though. Thanks for the water, that surely was a flaw in my plan."

"The mare's okay Sam?"

"Believe she'll be fine boss. Spent a bit of time with her, taking her around to investigate and get comfortable in the field. Though I still have no idea what spooked her so. I can't believe she remembered that field after twenty-two years. It has changed a lot since then. Why the whole farm has changed, grown bigger. You've made a real mark in the nurse mare market."

"We've made a mark Sam, and I couldn't have done it alone. Can you think of any other reason the Ghost would have acted that way, Sam?"

"Not really boss, but it can't be that. Horses are animals, and Ghost is not even as smart as most of the other horses. She is just a nurse mare."

"She did look at me like I betrayed her though, when she heard you leaving with Nellie. We couldn't leave her in the stall, like they do with the high dollar mares. Can you imagine what problems we would have had with all the horses when we took the foal away from her. I don't know about you, but I was afraid the other horses would tear the place down, when she began screaming, didn't you?"

"I sure did worry about that myself. Still, I wish I knew what the problem was; it was weird to be sure. Maybe we won't be able to breed her again. She is getting too old Sam?"

"How's Nellie, boss?" Sam asked.

"I moved one of the new mares into the Ghost's old stall. She won't be going back there anyway. Nellie seemed to be settling down; I hope there is no fall-out with her over the trouble this afternoon. I called the Vet, to make she is okay. I hope we will still need her milk, but if she foals much later, it will be out of season for nurse mares. She is old too. We may have to send her, and her foal to auction though. It's a good thing we kept that crop of fillies that were born four years ago. The price of mares has gone up. Goodness it costs even more to buy them now than it does to raise the fillies."

"It's hard isn't it boss? I mean to send them off to market after watching and caring for them for so many years? I know it's a part of the business, but it does get to one sometimes."

"Sam, even though I don't spend the kind of time around them that you do, what with all the bookwork and all, it's still hard. I can only imagine how it must be for you. I suspect you grow quite fond of some of them, don't you?"

"Yes boss, I do. But I also know you can't run a business keeping a lot of old nurse mares eating up the profit."

"When I started this business twenty-five years ago, I didn't know it would become this big of a business."

"There are a lot more people with show horses, and high-dollar mares than there used to be. Maybe it's just this new instant society we live in, and folks are just more impatient than they used to be boss?" Sam said as they neared the farm buildings.

Looking around the farm, Sam remembered the old days, when it consisted of a few fields for the horses. A couple of smallish barns, the house, and the garage. Observing it now, you wouldn't recognize that you were the same farm. Not if you hadn't seen the progression of progress made over the years.

In place of the two small barns there stood many small two stall barns, each stall had a paddock. Further away from the mares were the holding pens for the junk foals till they were shipped off to the buyers. He knew there were the farms that bought them, hand fed them for a bit and sold them. They went from there to the meat market, tanners, or the new crop of rescue leagues that were springing up. It mattered not, the farm didn't have to pay for their feed and nurturing and made a few coins on them to boot.

It was the nurse mares that were the prize. They had made the farm what it was today.

Of course, when the mares were nursing the prime foals they didn't live at the farm. There was no need of housing for them, thus enabling the farm to have more mares than it had stalls. Once the mare had given birth, and they took the foal away, the mare was shipped to the farm to live in style and nurse the new foal. It wouldn't come back to their farm until the high dollar foal was weaned, Sam thought as they pulled into the yard.

"Thanks again, Mr. Bentley for your help today. I'll get on with the rest of my chores as soon as I give a quick check on Nellie," Sam said as he got out of the truck.

"Sam, come on up to the house for supper. I will need to get your advice about the problem of my nephew, Tom."

"Sure boss," Sam said trying to fight off his disgust for the creep. He had an intense dislike for

lazy men and with a cruel streak it was unbearable
to Sam.

EIGHT

Sadie looked up from the bed of clover she was halfheartedly nibbling, and realized that Sam had left. It was nearly dusk, the sun on its way behind the hills, and she was alone in 'the field.' Unable to stop a tremble of fear she looked around again. *Maybe it will be okay this time,* she prayed.

She hoped the wolves were gone, but still feared as she felt her baby moving in her. She missed Nellie, just as she had missed her the first time, they were separated twenty-two years ago.

They were put in separate birthing fields then. All the birthing fields were quite far apart, and they were never near other horses; *they are always lonely places until the baby is born.* Sometimes she had an hour or two, and sometimes it was a day, to bond with her baby, before it was taken away. But the result was always the same, she'd lose her baby and she'd be taken to a new barn to nurse another's foal. As time went on, baby after baby was born, and lost to her, she held only dim memories of her friend Nellie and the fun days. *That is until they put us in adjoining stalls eleven months ago. What heaven it was to have an old friend to talk to again.*

I doubt I will see her again unless we meet at the auction. Sadie thought. I guess it's because the farm had grown so large, there were so many mares now, and they were both getting old.

Try as she might her mind continued to return to that night of terror when the wolves came.

Her baby had just been born, still attached by the umbilical cord. Both lying and resting. It hadn't even learned to stand yet when the wolves descended.

When the first wolf flew out of the woods with a howl, straight at the foal, she remembered screaming as it tore her baby from her, breaking the umbilical cord. Still weak from the birth, she got quickly to her feet and tried to fight, but the pack had descended. Already her baby was in pieces, the blood was everywhere, and the sounds of its little screams filled her ears even to this day, it sometimes haunted her dreams. During those nights she dreamt, and in her dreams, she watched again, and again the wolves drag parts of her baby away, before turning to her. It was too late for her baby, she fought for herself. The fight seemed to go on for hours. Finally, dawn broke, and the wolves slunk back into the forest. They too heard the truck coming up the rise.

The field was bloody from the fight, her neck had a large gash in it, one leg badly mauled, and the one wolf she had managed to kill with her hooves, lay on the ground near her.

She glanced nervously at the woods behind her and looked around the little field again. She didn't sense the wolves; *maybe they were gone*?

At least I have shelter now; she thought looking at the little run-in. It's a place to defend myself, and my baby from them if necessary. At least the trough is nearly inside the shelter.

The shelter was large as shelters went. She was glad for it and the security it would give. A chill breeze was coming through the trees now as night descended. *Soon it will be full dark.* She thought, as she watched the moon begin its slow movement in the sky overhead. *It is full tonight; there will be plenty of light to see quite a distance if need be.*

Still, horses aren't meant to be solitary creatures, and being alone gives me too much time to think.

NINE

The full moon and stars lit the April night so brightly; the mare could see the silhouettes of horses far off in the other fields. She would have joined them, but the fences were high and many, her belly heavy with the kicking foal.

Yesterday had been warm for early April. Now, the smell of rain was in the air, bringing with it a cold breeze in the predawn air. Feeling the changes in her body as the foal shifted position, she stood alone in the field with no herd to protect her or her baby from "the men."

Why can't I remember, I should be able to? Was it because of the wolves, she thought? Sadie looked around at the shadows; the trees in the distance looked menacing in the moonlight. Almost as if they might house a wolf pack. *I am older now I don't sense anything near that will harm my foal when it is born, and too young to defend itself.* The memory of that first foal still haunted her. *They circled me that night; I can still smell the musky, wild odor of them, as if it were yesterday, and not over twenty years ago.*

I know that many years have gone by. There have been many babies between then and now.

Still, it bothers me that I can't remember what sex that first baby was. Maybe I have blocked that memory! she thought.

Would she ever stop regretting it? Would it have been possible for me to save it, even though I was still so weak from birth? "Don't be silly Sadie; you were fragile, and young, no match for a pack of wolves." she told herself again.

If I had taught all my babies before they took them from me, would any of them be able to survive? Had they grown sturdy, and lived? Who had taught them? Did they ever have a chance? These questions daily tortured her mind and made her determined to start schooling early. "Goddess of Mares give me time to teach this one. He might be my last chance." The mare begged, knowing the time would be short before it too was taken.

A small brown bird landed at her feet, "Hello Ms. Cowbird." She said. The bird looked up at her, then down at the bits of hay scattered on the ground from last night's dinner. "Go ahead little one; I'm not going to eat it anyway. I am too near birth now to be hungry, and at least you are a bit of company. I am lonely tonight my friend." The bird looked up at her again questioningly and went back to eating. "You are up late tonight, but I'm glad for the companionship, little friend. I know that 'the men' aren't around or you wouldn't be here." Unafraid the bird looked at her again. *Cowbirds are a horse's friend,* she thought.

The shadows were deepening as the moon disappeared behind the clouds. The little bird looked up when it heard the hoot of an owl in the distance, and after taking one more morsel of hay, it flew off. *I can barely see the other horses now. I am truly alone now, without even the moon to keep me company,* Sadie thought. *I am trapped in this field, and in my memories tonight. I must indeed be getting old.*

Knowing, she would be tricked, drugged, and forced to accept another mare's foal. Her milk would help that other small life to grow and thrive. There were no illusions now; it had happened too many times before. If she didn't nurse the other mare's foal, they would sell her at auction or just put her down. She had seen it done with other mares when they refused. "Why would another mare want someone else to nurture her baby?' Sadie said, not understanding. 'This was not the way of the herd or the natural order of things. In nature, there were times when a mare died, and another mare nursed her foal; this was not the same."

The clouds were moving in, darkening, and hiding the stars, and moon, slowly they covered the sky. The frost on the grass in the pasture was melting; the mist is rising from the ground like a blue haze that made the field seem even more lonely.

TEN

So great is my anxiety tonight that my mind is retreating into the past, Sadie thought. I remember my second foal, the helplessness and fear I felt as the men tore it from my side, barely two days after it was born. I was so young and didn't understand. That was fourteen babies ago. I had been so grateful that the wolves hadn't come, that I wasn't afraid when the men showed up. I know better now.

"Why does my mind have to go back to all the hurtful things tonight, and so many years later too? First the wolves, then my second baby when I found out that the men didn't want my little one.' My mind won't let any of it go tonight. 'I was not quite four years old when they let the stallion in the paddock with the young mares." Sadie said to the clouds.

Since then, my life has been one of breeding and feeding. After I weaned each new one, I was given a week or two, to recuperate. Then, the stallion would be let loose in the mare's field again, and the cycle would start over.

Would the regret ever leave me for not teaching all those babies what they needed to know. Had they grown sturdy, and lived? Who had taught them? Had they ever had a chance? These questions tortured her mind daily, making her determined to start the schooling early, "Please give us time. This one might be my last chance," the mare begged, knowing the time would be short before it too was taken.

The men called her babies "junk foals," as if they had no importance. This is beyond understanding. My babies are as beautiful and smart as the foals they send me to nurse. "This time let me succeed when I fight to keep my baby," she whispered again to the clouds. I know it's hopeless; they will take this one away too. The only hope for it would be that her coaching would be enough to help it stay alive. Her determination was intense, to nourish, to love, and to teach this baby all that was possible in the little time they would have before 'the men' came.

Sometimes in dark moments, like tonight, her thoughts would turn to the lost babies, recalling the cries of the first, as 'the men' killed it before her eyes. At least, the men took all the other babies away. But I wonder, did any of them live and flourish. Had they grown up, and known love, or died without any chance of survival?

Now that I am over twenty, it is only a matter of time before I'll be unable to produce the milk these men want for the other foals. They will consider me of no use. Perhaps, they will put me out to pasture. More likely, my fate will be the auction or the meat market. What purpose will they have for a downtrodden old mare of ill-breeding when I cannot nurse the other foals?

ELEVEN

The darkness deepened, and she remembered. There were no colts in our small field, just us fillies. The giant oak tree sheltered us from the rain, and from the sun on swelteringly hot days. "Sarah,' I asked. 'Do you remember your mother?"

"A little Sadie,' she said. 'Not much but a little,"

Nellie piped in "I do, well I think I do. She was brown and white. At least I think she was, maybe it's just wishful thinking though. Do you, Sadie?"

"My mother was white," I said.

"Then why are you black?" Asked Nellie with Sarah nodding.

"I don't know why," I answered. The rain was still pouring even through the shelter of the giant oak, and we were getting soaked. Our heads began to droop lower no longer looking around with interest. We were too busy keeping the rain from our eyes. Soon the conversation stopped. It was okay to talk when it was drizzling, and we couldn't run or lie in the sun; but when it was raining buckets, we just stood there miserable and waiting, thinking to ourselves, *I expect we were all taken away from our mothers.*

After the rain had stopped, the scent of the sweet clover in the field caught our attention, and then we were off to play in the little patch of sand that we had worn clean of grass. Jumping and playing, our mothers forgotten at least for a time. When the wind came from the north, the smell of the cooking from the men's house would waft up into our nostrils. Other days we smelled the cows, the horses, the scent of wildflowers, and the pine trees. The trees loomed far off in the distance beyond many fields. Our field was in the center of many fenced in paddocks, to protect us from predators.

On a clear day, if we looked far off in the distance beyond the older horses' fields, we could see the empty fenced-in pastures nearer the pines. At times, there was a lone mare in one of these fields, and occasionally she would have a foal with her for a short time. We could see a shelter in the middle of these fields. It appeared that when a mare was there, she didn't leave it and go into the barn till her foal was gone. She looked so alone and frightened. None of us fillies wanted to speak of the mares, after the first time we saw one in those fields. It brought back memories that none of us wanted to face and made us all worry.

"Sadie, do you think that will be our fate?" Nellie asked me.

Looking at the little brown and white horse, I wondered.

"Did you hear something Nellie?" I asked.

"I think I heard the men say we would make nice nurse mares Sadie.' Nellie answered. 'Are they nurse mares?"

Pondering this for a minute, and trying to remember my mother, who I was sure now had been a nurse mare I said. "I think so, Nellie." Sarah crowded in, and the three of us stood in a tight circle afraid.

"Don't those mares look miserable, out there all alone?' Sarah said. 'Once I saw the men, go out to one of the fields, and drag the foal away. It was after I heard a thunderous noise that frightened me. When I looked toward it, I saw the mare on the ground. She wasn't dead though, for she stood up a little later, but her baby was gone then."

"I don't believe you, Sarah.' I said. 'Where were Nellie and I when that happened, if it is true?"

"Smarty pants,' Sarah said. 'I'm a bit older than you both; you weren't here yet. You will see one day." she said as she ran off. The rain had stopped, and the sun had come out, and Sarah was off to her favorite clover spot.

Sure, enough she was right. Early one morning the three of us were eating our breakfast in the little field when we saw 'the men,' walking out to the field where a mare stood with her new foal. As soon as the men got near the two, we heard a horrific noise that shattered the air. The mare fell to the ground, we watched her move a bit, and the men throw a rope around the foal's neck, carrying it off to the side. A gigantic red vehicle pulling a gray trailer drove over the short hill from the north.

After it stopped, the foal was flung into the back of it like it was a piece of garbage. Heads hanging low, and crying, we watched with heavy hearts as the mare got slowly to her feet, and the truck drove off. Looking at each other, tears in our hearts, we turned away and went back to eating. There was nothing we could do, and we had nothing to say to each other. We were all too alarmed.

One day we heard the men discussing a new colt that had been shipped off to auction.

"Do you suppose it will end up at the tanner's, the meat plant, or do you think some fool do-gooder, will rescue it?" the dirtiest of them asked the others. The other two grunted it didn't matter to them.

"What do we care, only some of the fillies have any importance. They might grow to be good nurse mares. That is if we require new nurse mares when they are born," the cleaner of the three said.

After they left, Nellie asked. "What is a nurse mare?" Sarah shrugged. I figured she didn't know either.

"What is a do-gooder then?" Sarah didn't answer.

I looked at Nellie, and whispered, "I don't know. All I know is that mares and some stallions are important, but only some of the fillies are important. I don't understand it all either, Nellie."

I was just as curious as she was, and I wanted to know what made one horse more important than another. It was as if our lives depended on knowing.

We were young and mostly happy in our little field, except for the times when the men came and checked our teeth and such. A year later the men came out to check us over and took Sarah away. We never saw her again. Nellie and I were terrified. "Where did they take Sarah?" Nellie asked me. I didn't have an answer. It was after that, that we began to shy away when anyone came into the pasture.

TWELVE

It wasn't until just before I was four that reality sunk in; the stallion was let loose in our field. Nellie and I were very frightened, he was so large and mean. It was no use. First one than the other of us got mounted. Soon Nellie and I were both with foal, and for a while we got extra food to eat and a larger field. How important we felt, yet the memory of Sarah never left us, and we worried. What had happened to Sarah? Why had they taken her away? What had they seen when they looked in her mouth that day?

As we grew big with our foals, Nellie and I watched the far-off fields more closely. Would we be one of those mares soon?

How young we were to believe that we had importance beyond our milk. We found out soon enough though. We learned what those fields were for. As one by one, we were taken from our little area, separated, and put alone for the first time in what would become our birthing field.

Wolves killed my first baby. It was the most horrifying and awful experience I remember. I will never forget the smell of their wet musky fur, the growls, and yelps as they tore my baby away from me as I lie weakly on the ground after giving birth. I watched and screamed as they ripped its young throat open and its belly apart, tearing out its entrails and watching the blood flow onto the ground. The men came too late with their guns, but I heard them say, "No matter, it was a boy, just another junk foal. It is a good thing that the other foal is already born. We don't have to worry about her milk drying up on us." I stood in shock, what were they saying? *My baby had just been killed, half of it dragged off into the woods by the wolf pack!*

"Ben, you had better give her something or her milk will be useless, and we might lose her from shock," I heard the bearded man say in a disgusted tone.

"Good idea Sam, you are thinking tonight," Ben said as he stuck a needle into my neck. Soon I felt sleepy and could barely stand as they led me onto the horse trailer. The lights were bright and hurt my eyes when I awoke in a stall with a foal next to me, eating hungrily. At first, I wanted to push this foal away, screaming where is my baby? Then I smelled the birthing fluids on it. *Maybe my baby hadn't been killed by wolves. Maybe it was a dream I told myself.*

"She is taking to the new foal nicely," I heard Ben say to Sam. Looking up I realized that the wolves weren't a bad dream. My baby was dead; it was true. Again, I was angry. Then looking down at this little boy that I had been feeding for two days I sighed. Even though my heart was still breaking for my own little one, I had bonded, and couldn't be cruel to this little life that trusted me. It looked to me as if I was its mother. *I will mourn my baby later,* I thought.

Nurturing and loving this new little life, I wondered why it was so much more important than my baby had been. Men and women came to the stall and cooed and cawed over it. They brushed us both and gave me the first full combing I had ever had. They cleaned my feet and trimmed my hooves more often too. No germs were allowed in with the new foal. For a while, I felt deep love and care for both the humans and the little foal, until one day I found myself back in my field alone. The foal was off in the distance in the foal's field, running and playing. It was happy and I was alone, without even Nellie to keep me company.

All too soon, they put me back on the trailer and took me to the old barn. Now I couldn't even watch the little foals anymore.

No one brushed me anymore. My feet weren't cleaned or trimmed as often. The loneliness only lasted for a few days, before they put me into a field with a bunch of other mares and let that big, mean stallion in our field again. He was all black with a golden tail and mane, and only fought the men until he smelled us mares.

Once he smelled us, it was all the men could do to keep him under control long enough to get him through the gate into our field. Again and again he brutally took each of us, until he was spent, and then they put the stallion in the trailer and took him away.

From year to year the plants changed a bit, the trees grew taller and some were cut back, and a little shelter now stood in the center of the field where I went with the other nurse mares when the days got particularly nasty. Nothing must happen to our milk. It is unimportant to the 'men' what happens to our babies, except to make sure that we give birth so that we get in milk. If our baby is a filly, sometimes they keep them, and we at least get to nurse them and see them in the little filly field for a while. *I guess that is why they have extra nurse mares. Just in case one has a filly, and they decide to keep it for breeding. Though that only happens when other nurse mares are getting too old to breed or are heavy with their last baby.*

Though we were too far away to speak to them or nuzzle them, even if we remembered which one ours was, I remembered which one mine was the first time I saw her in the little field with the other fillies. Even though I was once again with foal, I fought to get to her. *I still wanted to teach her, and at least give her love before she grew to suffer my fate.* But the men took me further out and away from that little field so that I could no longer see her.

After that, I pretended to ignore the fillies when the men were around. At least I could watch some of the little ones grow up. Not the boys though, they never lived on our farm. What happened to them? I wondered. Sometimes, I could see Nellie off in the distance, and on a good day when the wind blew just right, we called back and forth to each other for a minute or two.

TWELVE

With a racing heart and sweat pouring from her, the foal began his journey down the birth canal. The noise was deafening. He could feel the stress and fear of his mother, feel her body cramping, and repositioned himself as the tightening of her muscles pushed him out of the warm dark haven, he had been in for so many months. First the front hooves, then head and shoulders broke through into the cold April air. Just as the rain started, he took his first breath. Soon only his back hooves remained in the birth canal, and both mare and foal lay there resting, connected yet apart.

I watched him as he tried to catch all the sights and smells of this new world as rapidly as possible; and when he eagerly pulled himself along the dew-covered ground away from me, I chuckled.

How handsome he is, all black with a white blaze on his forehead. Gazing at him, with love she licked him clean and watched for predators. "You are beautiful and smart. You must listen to me if you are to stay alive. First, you must learn to stand."

Sadie watched as he put his legs under himself and tried to rise, and each time he fell he tried again. Soon his small legs held his weight. Though it was many attempts, and many more falls, before he finally stood firmly.

"Your stomach is growling little one."

Forgetting the past, I watched him searching, and finding, the source of the smell that made his belly hurt. Finally, he took the first drink of her milk.

Dawn broke. *Even through the heavy cloud cover, the bright light hurt his eyes, so used to the darkness of the womb.* Birds were chirping overhead. A light drizzle fell, melting the last of the white frost that had covered the grass. The delight watching his growing curiosity gave me hope, and joy. Hungry again, he fed as I taught him about each new thing he saw.

"Little one, look at the herd over there in that field, watch how they play together. Do you see how the alpha mare finds the best food for her herd? Can you see the alpha male standing watch as the others graze, and play? It is his job to protect the herd from predators, the same as it is the alpha mare's job to find the best food."

"Listen carefully. It might be your job to protect the herd from coyotes and wolves when you grow up. Men can also be terrible predators, though I have heard that some of them are excellent friends to horses. I don't have personal experience with that, so don't judge all men by what you may see and learn in the beginning, son. I hope you are blessed little one, and find a home, and humans who love you and understand horses."

She filled his mind with pictures of strange bugs and told him which ones would bite and which would only pester.

"I've taught you about bugs, what is good for horses to eat, and what is not. Now, I need to speak about humans, or at least as much as I know or have heard. Some humans believe all animals, including horses, are dumb, and they consider us property to do with as they wish.

Lately, I have overheard the humans talking about other humans that wish to help horses, and care about them. They call them do-gooders. The fortunate thing about them is they are taking in nurse mare foals and finding them forever homes. I know you will find a forever home. You must remember that for times will be hard for you at first."

"I won't leave you, momma."

"Sweet boy, I fear the men may force a separation on us, and way too soon for you too."

"Why?"

"That is something I don't understand, little one. But it happens. There is something else you must remember: whether we like it or not change happens. We must roll with it and do our best to accept those things we cannot yet change and change the things we can."

"I don't understand."

"I expect you don't, little one. But one day you may remember my words, and perhaps it will help you. So much of what happens in a herd or with humans will depend on what you give, and how you act toward each of them."

His young brain took it all in as he listened, even to those things that didn't make any sense. Somehow, he knew it was essential for him to be taught. At times his mind wandered. Then with a nudge or a nip, he would once again pay attention.

"If you are to grow strong and tall, you must eat, young one. You are fine-looking and will learn to survive if you listen to me. Keep in mind, that you will find a home and love. Hold on to that during the hard times," she told him repeatedly, praying that it would be true.

THIRTEEN

The rain has stopped. The frost is gone from the grass leaving behind a sweet wet aroma. It smells wonderful. Why does the smell of the grass, and the sun growing higher make mother reek of fear, and terror, he wondered? Always watchful now, her head moves *back, and forth rapidly. Her mind-pictures are now of strange, two-legged creatures coming. Why is she afraid of them? It's far too much for me to absorb. The images are beyond anything I know, and I can't discern what they mean.*

It is late afternoon. The moon has come and gone twice. I've eaten, napped, and listened to her stories many times. Feeling mother's dread getting stronger, I wondered, what was about to happen, and when it would happen?

"Mom, what is happening? Why are you worried?"

No answer, she just continued to pace around me, nuzzling, licking, nipping, loving, trying to shelter me. As the odor of her panic grew stronger, her milk tasted acidy, not sweet like it had been the day before or in the predawn light.

Far off in the distance, she began watching the large brown block that stood beyond the fence. Even though I did not understand the source of her fright, I knew it would come from there.

It was nearly dawn when I saw the small two-legged creatures that looked almost like ants. They're coming from the direction of the brown block. Were they the source of her dread? I didn't ask, knowing she wouldn't answer now. The closer they came, the stronger their stench became. They didn't smell at all like mother; they reeked of things I didn't understand.

Were they the human predators that she had told me were a danger to horses? What, and who were they? Moving in front of me, ears back, puffed up ready for a fight she smelled of danger.

The movements of the 'men' sounded like thunder as they drew closer. Clumsily they walked on those two legs of theirs. One of them is carrying something long, and black. What is it? The closer they came, the bigger they appeared, and the smaller mother seemed to become. Dejected, yet still ready to fight for me, she reared up in desperation.

"Please, let me keep this one. He is extraordinary," she cried.

I pushed my little boy behind me, I knew that his belly would be aching with hunger, but I couldn't protect him if he were nursing. "Mommy, why won't you let me eat? Is it those smelly creatures coming toward us?"

"Shush little one, remember I love you," I said as I ran at the men, looking like a wild demon. "You do not frighten me. I will fight you or die trying," I screamed at the men.

One of the men yelled. "Drug her!" The other held up the long black thing he carried. Out of it came a loud horrific noise. Frightened I sensed my little one turn to flee.

"Mommy." He yelled as he watched my legs wobble as I fell slowly to the ground. I could feel his fear, and his eyes on the feather sticking out of me and knew he would try to get back to my side. "Mommy, what's wrong? Please don't be dead."

My chest still rose and fell, but all I could do was gaze at my baby. A horrible sadness filled me, as our eyes met for the last time, and I whimpered "I love you little one." in a desperate goodbye, as I watched the men picked him up, and carry him away from me.

They put a rope around his neck and held him. One of the men held one of those small black things that humans are always using, close to his mouth. In a rough voice, he said, "Come in, we are ready."

Lying on the ground, still unable to stand, I watched how petrified he was. I was so proud of him! As small as he was, he still tried to fight. *Don't hurt my baby*, I thought, and prayed he would find a home and not be killed or left to die.

As the trailer came into view over the horizon, I knew that he would think it a monster with its loud growling noise. I hadn't had time to explain about men's trucks, and how they stank and rolled on wheels. *How would my little one even hope to understand something that didn't walk on two legs or four? Nor fly like the birds or crawl on the ground like the worms and bugs.*

I yelled as loudly as I could "Little One, don't be frightened. I know it smells of smoke, and oil, fear, and death." It is coming closer, and closer, finally it stopped. *I will die from his agony and fear,* I thought, as I realized he was sobbing and that he recognized he was too small to fight them. He did not know how to puff up, and rear, and if he did it wouldn't help with these men. *How desperate my baby is, already alone, and just learning how helpless he is.*

Still, I struggled to get up as I watched them pick him up and toss him into the back of the trailer as if he were a piece of meat. As the doors closed on him, I heard him scream "Mommy!"

I will not nurse another mare's foal, no matter how sweet, and hungry it is. My heart is broken, crestfallen, head hanging low, still weeping, Sadie thought. I will find a way to help Nellie and her baby.

FOURTEEN

Watching as the beat-up old trailer drove off with my beautiful little boy, I cried. Would I be able to keep my word to myself, and not nurse another foal? I didn't know if I'd be able to, between the drugs and the tricks men pulled. Maybe this time they will not need me, perhaps another mare will have the job, and I will be sent to auction with Nellie. I must help Nellie and her little one. They must not die. Oh, please let my baby find a home and love.

All too soon another trailer pulled up, and Samuel led me onto it. I did not look at him. I would never meet his eyes again, nor trust him. *Were there, as I had heard, humans who understood horses, and cared for them?*

The drug still hung in my system, the trailer moved off, and all too soon we were at the new barn. *I can't help Nellie, and her little one if I am here nursing another foal for six months. What can I do?* Providence took hold, A woman came out of the house and was speaking low to Samuel. He didn't look happy with what she was telling him, but soon he shook her hand, nodded, and walked back to the truck. Jackson had already opened the trailer and had begun to walk me out when Samuel came back. "Jack put her back in and close the door; we will be going back to the barn. I don't know what the boss will want us to do with the Ghost. She is too old to be kept around for breeding."

"Boss, what happened?" Jackson asked as he closed the trailer.

"They had another mare already. Mrs. Cruthers told me that one of the boarder's mares gave birth, and the baby died. Usually, under these circumstances, they would have either let the mare nurse her foal or gotten another nurse mare for her. But the owner's daughter was away at college and not going to be showing that year, so they offered her mare as a nurse mare to the other foal. It was a win-win for the stable. Unfortunately for us, they have no use for the Ghost."

"I know its business boss, but how shitty of them. After all, we had a contract. Did you remind them of that?"

"No Jack, I knew the boss wouldn't want me to alienate a future client. We will take our losses this year."

At that, the door closed, and I couldn't hear them anymore.

As awful as the 'I don't know what we will do with the Ghost,' sounded I would not be nursing another's foal. Just maybe I could help Nellie and her baby, and I could look for my baby.

As we drove away from the barn, my spirits lifted. I didn't want to fall in love with someone else's foal. I didn't want to break my promise to Nellie or at least die trying. I know that Nellie won't see me, and I won't go back to the big beautiful stall I had been in but be put out into some field for a bit. It may be a day or a week, but I'd be sent to auction. The probability was strong that Nellie would also be sent to auction, and with her foal still inside of her. It would be my job to help them if I could.

Horses talk. It is possible that she will hear that I have been sent back, if not from the other horses, then she will hear it from one of the farm hands. It will give her hope. It gave me confidence. I knew this could help me that I would be able to help, Nellie, her baby, or even myself. We might all die, but we could try.

Day turned into night, the men came, and threw a bit of hay into the small fenced in paddock. *This wasn't a regular field or paddock, but more of a holding pen,* I thought. I heard them grumbling. "What is the use of wasting hay on this old mare anyway? We will be sending her and the other ones to auction in a couple of days."

"That's a stupid question. The boss won't get a thing for a scrawny, hungry thing. She's too old to breed, her coat is none too promising for the tanner, so she will probably be shipped off to Mexico and sold to the slaughter house. They still eat horse meat there."

"OH!!"

"Besides we have a lot of new fillies ready for breeding this year."

"About how many are going to auction, Doug?"

"I expect about fifteen or twenty, but the boss would know for sure. We will find out when the time comes."

I barely heard their last words as they got into the hay wagon. But I knew my fate, and that of Nellie and her baby. I had a day or two to put together a plan. The questions would be, would

Nellie and I find each other, and would the plan work? But first I had to come up with a plan.

The sky was black with no moon, and the cloud covered the stars tonight; but still I could see, as horses do. I wandered around listening to the sound of the owls, and the far-off cries of the coyotes, and thought.

FIFTEEN

At dawn, the trailers pulled up. Nellie and about fifteen other mares were led into the paddock. We ignored each other until everyone was unloaded and the trailers drove off.

"Oh Sadie, what happened?" Nellie asked as soon as the trailers were gone. By then I had a crowd of mares surrounding me, listening, waiting for me to speak.

"They took my baby, Nellie. He was so beautiful, and smart too. I tried to fight them."

"There is no way to fight the 'men'," someone in the back yelled.

"But, why are you here? Why aren't you off nursing?" Nellie asked.

"The stable didn't need me. It seems that another mare lost her baby, and she was nursing the new foal."

"Why are we all here?" another voice asked.

I hadn't met these other mares yet, so I didn't know who was talking. Still, I answered. "I don't know for sure."

"Oh God, Sadie, not the auction?" Nellie cried.

"Maybe, but perhaps we will be sent somewhere else,' I said, not wanting to get everyone in a panic. Not yet; and if my plan were to work, we would need all of us. We must wait until after they bring us our hay, and then we must plan. 'I don't think we have much more than a day or two. Let's all eat and get to know each other. That way we can exchange ideas better."

"I don't want to die," a big brown mare cried from the crowd.

"None of us want to die. What's your name?"

"I used to be called Sandy, but the men just call me mare."

"Hi Sandy, this is Nellie, and I am Sadie, though the men have been calling me Ghost since I turned white about three years ago. Before that, they called me mare, or the gray one. I guess of all of us here in the group, Nellie is the only one that has always called me Sadie."

"My filly name was Aronka," a smaller black mare yelled.

For a while we all learned each other's names, as we moved from hay pile to hay pile. It was cramped, and the hay scarcer than any of us were used to, but it was something.

Soon, it was Nellie and me, standing at the fence. Every tiny scrap of hay was gone, and most of the mares were in small groups, some napping, others murmuring, and some were crying softly.

"What are we to do Sadie?"

"I've been thinking about just that, Nellie, but am unsure of telling everyone yet. How many of these other mares do you know?"

"Just a couple, Sadie. I never met most of them, though I could see them off in other fields sometimes. I met Aronka before, but since she has some Arabian blood she can be skittish. The gray over in the corner comforting Pippi is Bonnie. Pippi can be trusted, she's quiet, and usually a calming force. Bonnie isn't that old but has gone barren. Do you have a plan, Sadie?"

"I think so, Nellie. "From what I saw at auction when we were fillies, they put a group into a small pen like this and sell them as a lot."

"What do you mean by a lot, Sadie?"

"They don't go on the auction block, but someone bids for the entire bunch of horses."

"That doesn't sound very positive for any of us Sadie."

"It isn't Nellie. The horses are penned very tightly and can hardly move around in those pens."

"What will we do? Is my baby not even going to be born, Sadie, but die in some slaughter house while it's still inside of me?"

"Not if I can help it, Nellie. Not if my plan works."

"What is your plan, Sadie?"

"Please don't spread it around yet, we need to get a real feel for everyone. I think from what you have said, we can let Pippa in on the plan, and perhaps she will know of a few more that can be told. Everyone else must wait until we are at the auction."

"I'll go talk to Pippa now, while Bonnie is napping. Perhaps she will know of a few more we can tell."

"Tell her to meet us over in the corner when the rest of the mares are napping. I don't want to chance they don't feed us in the morning but come with trailers instead."

With that, Nellie sauntered off toward Pippa, stopping here and there to give a comforting word to one of the mares. *Nellie was smart; if she'd gone directly over to Pippa, it would have caused too much curiosity among the rest.*

SIXTEEN

A bit later Nellie came back, followed shortly by Pippa and Misty. They moved quietly through the sleeping mares, not wishing to cause any alarm in the others.

"This is Misty. Mona and Poppy will be alright to help, but I think it better if we don't all stand around together."

"That is smart thinking Pippa. Hi Misty. I am Sadie, and this is Nellie."

"What's the plan, Sadie."

"At the auction, those who aren't of prime stock are generally penned together and sold as a lump to some foreign buyer. They aren't brought up to the auction block for bidding but sold as a package. I know it sounds awful, and it's probably worse than it even sounds, but this time could very well suit our purpose."

"How can it suit our purpose? Pippa asked.

"We'll have to arrange for all the horses in the pen to stampede, making sure that they know they can't stay together as a herd if they value their lives. But they must split into small groups of one or two. Everyone will need to go in a different direction. We will need to be prepared to run, and run fast, and get away from all the other horses as fast as we can go."

"Sadie that is going to be a tough one. Horses run in herds, it's our instinct."

"Pippa, that is the hardest part, making sure no one stays in a group. None of the mares can follow their instincts and remain in a herd. If they do, they will be caught for sure. We may be caught anyway, and some of us might die. But some of us might survive and find a home or a place to live out our lives in the wild."

"I can talk to Kit Kat, Molly, Poppy, and Bella. They are trustworthy. I know that we will need to tell everyone, but I think you are right, this must be done in a way that as many of us as possible have a chance to live. There are a few here that will act up too quickly if they know ahead of time," Misty said quietly.

"I'll talk to Lady, Rosie, Lillie, Autumn, and Dolly. That will only leave three or four that don't know the plan yet, but I think it best that I tell Bonnie when we are on the trailer, and Misty can tell Aronka. Those of us who know will fill in the rest. I fear for some of them. I don't know they will be able not to follow their instincts, but perhaps if we partner up, we can do it."

"Yes, that sounds like a plan. No more than three horses going off together, better for us all if we can do it in pairs, but we must go in different directions. Oh yes, tell everyone that if they find water, to make sure they travel a bit in it. It will make it harder to track them; and to stay away from any human until they are a long way from the auction."

Before dawn, Pippa and Misty wandered off, each of them stopping to speak to a different mare for a bit, before walking off.

"Nellie it will be hardest for you, carrying the foal. Do you think you can stay with me for your baby's life? Do you think you will be able to run? Oh, not for a long time, but a bit?"

"Sadie, I am strong, and I will make it. I won't falter. I will run, I don't know for how long I will be able to, but I will run. With you at my side, we will make it, and keep my baby well."

"Nellie, we will have to find a way to hide from the searchers. I hope there is water near, for both drinking and hiding our scent; and there must be trees, a lot of them too. I know I'm putting a lot of hope out in the winds tonight...."

"It is the best plan we can make, Sadie. Now let's get a bit of rest, so we are up to the next step."

"Good idea," I said yawning.

SEVENTEEN

The mares huddled in small groups as dawn broke. Pippa, Misty, Nellie, and I sailed between the groups, giving the appearance of chatting, plans made, and partners picked. Pippa and Misty had done as they promised during the night, and all but a few knew the plan.

Most of the mares had picked a partner. It appeared that no hay would be delivered today, so Aronka, Bonnie, and the others were being filled in on the plan by those who knew them best and could convince them that it was the best plan.

It appeared that the last few would be included in groups of three, with two strong-willed mares to keep them going even should they become too afraid or frozen with fear at the last moment; or worse yet, instead of fleeing with their partners, tried to become a herd as was our instinct. It would be death if they stopped thinking and followed their instinct that the more of them there were, the safer they would be. When in fact this would be the least safe for any of them.

I hope they all make it. I know I've done what I can to help them all, Sadie thought. But I will be focused on Nellie and her baby. I will make sure that no one follows us. Humans don't realize horses can be smart too and deter from what is their supposed normal behavior. How sad it is that we are considered meat now, and of no use to anyone. As if our lives and those of our lost babies had no importance except to enrich humans, or for the pleasure and delight of humans.

The head of every mare in the field rose at the first drone of the engines. They knew what was coming even before they could see the trailers.

"Remember everyone, do not fight now. Do not give the 'men' the chance to be wary of us. If you do, we will not survive this." Sadie yelled loudly.

"What do we do if there are no trees?" asked Miriam.

"Run in, and around houses or buildings, until you can lose the humans, and get to trees," Sadie answered.

"What kind of fencing will they have? yelled Kit Kat.
"If we are lucky, they will be wood or even electric. Electric stings a bit, but if you run fast, it breaks it quickly," shouted Pippa.

"If it's metal then what?" Bonnie cried.

"The last one off the truck must stop in at the gate long enough for us to all charge and go through the gate. If it is you, turn around, fight with all your might; and if you must, run like the whip is on your back, even if you have a rope on your neck.' Misty answered. 'Do not lose your partners, stay close to them at all times. It is your life and all our lives you are fighting for. If you are the last, and the fencing is metal, you might not make it. All of us will go to slaughter if you don't stop them from closing the gate."

"If it's metal and short fencing, jump it if you can as soon as the last mare is blocking the gate. If I am last, I will buck or rear, turn, and run, rope or no rope around my neck. Make sure you are all as close to the gate as possible whether it is metal or not," added Pippa. 'Take no chances, don't look spooked, but as if you were crowding because you were looking for comfort. And again, I tell you. Stay close to your partners."

Sadie and Nellie stood quietly. Pippa, and Misty knew these mares best and were strong enough to handle it.

"But the men are so big, and strong" cried Aronka.

"If we are just one or two that is true; but if it is all of us, and they aren't expecting it, I don't think they will be able to stop a stampede."

The trucks and trailers stopped, and a hush fell over the field. The mares' heads all fell, and they appeared beaten, and meek to the eyes of the humans who arrived in the trailers. The chilly night turned into a misty, cloudy day, almost as if the sky were crying for the mares.

The men began roping the mares. The mares did not scatter but stayed with their partners and gave the appearance of being downtrodden and resigned. The men led each group up the ramp and into the trailer. When the first trailer was filled, it pulled off, and the second loaded. For a moment, Bonnie and Aronka started to put up a hissy fit but were quickly calmed by Pippa and Misty.

"Hey Joe, where is Samuel today?"

"He doesn't like this part Jack. I think he gets a bit attached to the mares."

"A little squeamish?"

"Yah probably, but don't let him hear you say that, or you will be out of a job. He's the boss, so I guess he decides who does what." I sure wish we didn't have to have Tom come with us today. I dislike that man."

"Me too, Jack. He's got a real cruel streak, is dumb as a dishrag, doesn't listen to anyone, stinks to high heaven, and the worst thing is he is afraid of horses."

"Let's let him mind the gate as we bring the mares into the pen."

"Good idea, since he doesn't have that crop anymore. It is probably the safest thing for him to do."

"The mares are very quiet today. I was expecting a bit of a fight with some of them, Joe."

"Yah me too, but I guess they've been around long enough that they are resigned."

"They are just dumb animals, Joe."

EIGHTEEN

Each mare played her part well. Not one of the humans could suspect that a plan was afoot.

Looking out of the small window, Sadie thought, *how small that little pen was, without a speck of grass or clover underfoot.* "I'm hungry Sadie, are you?" Nellie asked.

"Yes Nellie, I am. I expect we will not have a meal today. With luck, we will find something when we escape. Your baby needs the food, and it will be harder for us to run and hide if we are hungry. Though I expect the men don't care, we are too close to the auction for them to waste the feed on us."

"I'm terrified, Sadie."

"Me too. But the plan must work. It just must. If it doesn't, we are all dead anyway. I don't want to die or for you and the baby to die. Although, I am happy I am here with you instead of nursing another's foal, and then going to my death alone, knowing that you went to yours without me to help."

"I don't know how I would have managed without you, dear friend. I have never been a planner; you know that about me. I've always lived in the moment and tried to forget the bad things. But I'm not ready to die, and I want my baby. I wish you also had your baby late, and perhaps we could both have saved ours. I'm going to keep believing your last baby finds a home, a family, and a herd to belong to."

"Thank you, Nellie, I am praying for that. Perhaps the Gods will be good to him and help him."

The drone of the truck continued, with the mares crowded in and bumping against each other on every turn the trailer made. Sadie protected Nellie with her body as best she could, but even still there were times her friend got jostled. *This is not good for the baby,* she thought.

Even though the April day was cold, the horses quickly became overheated from the stuffy confines of the trailer. Nellie's sweating became worse. The trailer stank from the waste from so many mares locked in it.

Soon they could all hear the noise of humans on the grounds around them, and the smell of fear from the other horses at the auction added to their dismay.

"Oh God, Sadie, the fences are the tall metal ones."

"We are in the last trailer Nellie, and in the back of it. I'm going to try to be the last out. With luck, you will be taken out just before me. They won't expect much from me. I've been nearly invisible to them for twenty-odd years now. I will buck, rear, and run. Somehow when we are safe, we will need to get the rope off me, but I'll try to pull it into my mouth for a bit Nellie."

"Oh Sadie, why us? Why does it have to be the metal ones? And there are so many buildings before the trees."

"We can and will do this, Nellie. I hope everyone else can get free too, but I'm concentrating on you and your baby Nellie. If we go toward the buildings, you won't have to run as far. Once we are behind the buildings, the tree line is very close. I think the humans will be watching the rest of the mares, and on this cloudy, rainy day, we will be able to escape more easily."

"We will make it Sadie. Somehow, someway we will do it."

"They've started unloading the first trailer, Nellie, and the mares are going in quietly and standing as close to the gate as they can in smallish groups. We can do this! The pen is a bit bigger than even I hoped, so it will give us all some running room."

"Well we are up; Manny has already headed for home with his trailer. Let's start our unloading, Jack."

Sadie and Nellie watched as the mares were led into the pen one by one. So, rank had the trailer become from the waste and fear of the mares that it was almost a pleasure to get off, even though they all knew the fight that was yet to come.

Rain began to come down quite hard now, and the cloud cover made it difficult to see well.

"Nellie, the rain and clouds will help us all, as long as we don't slip in any mud. Luckily it has been very dry lately, so it will take a long time for it to get muddy. Do you see that group of buildings over by the tree line?"

"Yes, is that the way you want us to go?"

With a quiet nicker, Sadie indicated yes. The men had begun to unload their trailer now.

"Nellie, we are going to weave in and out of those buildings, and make for the trees," Sadie said in a whisper.

"Why don't we go in the other direction? There are no buildings, just trees off in the distance."

"I fear there is too much open ground that way. Besides I expect when the stampede starts, nearly all the other mares are going to head that way. It will be too easy to be rounded up if they are all going in that direction." *Oh please, whoever is listening, help us*, Sadie thought.

All too quickly, Nellie was led off the trailer, and Joe had a rope around Sadie's neck. As meekly as she could, Sadie stood quietly head down. *Don't give them any trouble now,* she thought, as she was led down the ramp.

As planned the mares were crowded near the gate. No amount of shooing back would get them to budge.

"Joe, I haven't been to an auction before, do the horses always stay by the gate like that?" Jack asked.

"Not always, I admit it's quite strange, but they all seem to be very quiet, and resigned, so I'm not going to worry about it. We only have the Ghost to get into the pen, and we are done."

"Who's going to collect the money for them after they are sold, Jack?"

"Oh, the auction house will send it over to the boss later. They do a lot of business here. There is no need to worry. As soon as we have them in the pen, I'm going to get into the truck, go back to the farm, and have a nice cold beer."

NINETEEN

Okay Sadie old girl, you are down the ramp now, get your courage up. Remember your lost babies and Nellie's baby. You can do this and live to help Nellie too. At least the rope is a short one, and it is not even tied. It won't get tangled up in my feet, and it will probably come off when I rear. That cruel man Tom is minding the gate. In a way that is a good thing. He is afraid of horses; he'll leap out of the way quickly enough. Lordy, he'll probably land on his ass.

"Tom open the gate inward, not outward. How many times do I have to tell you that?" Jackson yelled.

"Mind your mouth, Jackson. I heard you the first time." Tom screamed, spittle running down his mouth.

"God, he looks like he's foaming at the mouth now, Jack. I'm sure glad we are nearly done, and that it's the Ghost who is last. She is so mild mannered you never worry about her," he said, walking Sadie down the ramp, the rope hanging loosely around her neck.

As they walked up to the gate, Tom pulled it outward again, with a smirk on his face, and he took a bow. At that moment, Sadie reared, and with a flying leap, turned, and ran, with Nellie on her heels. The rest of the mares stampeded out of the gate all of them going in different directions. They galloped as fast as they could go, none losing sight of their partners.

Jack flung himself to one side when Sadie reared, and the stampede began. Tom, lay on the muddy ground, curled into as small of a ball as he could get, sweat pouring down his face. The pounding of hooves filled his ears; his eyes shut tight, he clung to the side of the fencing. His worst nightmare had become his reality.

Crowds of men and women, who once were walking among the paddocks viewing the horses, flew in every direction almost as if they had wings.

No guns were allowed on the property; no one was prepared for the ruckus. Not a soul had ever seen anything like this happen in their lives.

And the mares ran. Groups of two or three mares headed off toward the tree line, none of them joining the others but staying with their partners, and they flew across the field. Before any human could get into a truck, the mares had disappeared into the woods.

Sadie and Nellie went as fast as they could in the other direction, straight for the buildings, weaving in and out of them as quickly as possible. The tree line was closer behind these buildings than it was on the other side.

As Sadie had predicted, everyone was watching the other mares fly over the field toward the woods and didn't notice her and Nellie in the rain.

Luckily the rope came off when I reared, Sadie briefly thought, and then watched their path. They had made it to the trees and slipped into the woods with none the wiser for their going.

"Can you make it a bit further, Nellie?" Sadie asked, the wind taking the sound of her voice to her friend.

"The baby and I are okay Sadie. We need to put some more distance between us and the humans, don't we?"

"It would be best; we aren't safe yet. I smell water. Do you?"

Sniffing the air, Nellie whinnied a positive response.

"When we get to the water, we must drink as we wade upstream. We can't slow down enough to eat or even get a proper drink yet. Will you be okay with that?"

"Yes!!"

The sound of rushing water filled their ears as they got closer to it. So fast were they traveling, they nearly fell in before they saw it. A quick drink was all they took before they waded in and began moving upstream, staying as close as possible to the plants and trees along the bank.

The day became night, and then day again. They stopped along the edge of the river, ate a bit, napped, and drank their fill. As the sky began to lighten, the two of them moved into the river again. "I think we must be at least fifty or sixty miles away by now, maybe even more. We've been traveling for three days. Do you think they will find us now?" Nellie asked.

"I don't think so, but we need to start looking for either a mossy area or a rocky one."

"Why's that Sadie?" Nellie asked.

"We should take to the hills. Can you hear the river? We are coming up on some small rapids. But we don't want our tracks to show."

"Sadie, how do you know so much about tracks?"

"Do you remember when the vet came last? He was talking about the old days and having to hide his tracks when he was out fishing."

"I sort of remember that conversation, but didn't understand why he'd need to do that?"

"From what I remember it was something about other fisherman not following him to the best fishing spots. But I mostly remember him saying he had to stay on the moss or walk over rocks. Nellie, we must find some moss or rocks soon though."

"The water is getting colder Sadie; I don't like it."

"I suspect it's because we are getting closer to the hills, and further north Nellie. You watch that side, and I'll watch this side.

"Sadie!!! I see some mossy rocks ahead."

"I see them too. Do you think you can climb them, Nellie?"

"They don't look too steep. We'll just have to watch our footing and take it slowly. They might be a bit slick from the water. Oh no, Sadie, I think the baby is coming." Nellie said just as they reached the rocks.

"Hang in there Nellie. After we get over the rocks, we'll find a safe clearing in the woods. I'll stay behind you and give you a boost with my head. I can see that your body is getting ready to have the baby."

TWENTY

As the two mares climbed up onto the mossy rocks, Nellie needed to go to the bathroom more frequently. Luckily, the woods were very close now, and Nellie was still very restless. *It's a good thing that Nellie is so good natured*, Sadie thought. *If she was the cranky type, I don't know if we'd make it. But perhaps all this exercise and her desperation to save her baby has helped her to stay calmer. She is so sweaty; I hope this isn't harming her baby.*

"Look, Nellie; there is a little meadow just a bit higher on the hill. It's pretty sheltered from the weather and human eyes."

"I see it. Thank the Gods.' Nellie said, waddling behind her friend. 'It's getting harder to walk, Sadie."

Just as they reached the little glen, the sun peeked out of the clouds. "Over here, Nellie.' Sadie said leading her friend to a small area under a canopy of trees. 'You can rest now. We will stay here until your baby can walk with us."

Without a word, Nellie laid down on the soft grass; her belly extended now. It was only a few minutes before her water broke, when they heard the children.

"I can't go anywhere now Sadie; the baby is coming."

"It'll be okay Nellie. I think we are far enough away unless they turn us over to the auction again."

"Rebecca, look a mare is giving birth over there.' Noah said to his sister. 'Run get Papa. I've helped with the foaling before; I'll stay here."

"Okay, Noah," Rebecca yelled back, as she turned and ran toward the farm.

"Shush girls, everything will be okay now. I'm here, and Papa will be here soon. We will all help you."

The sound of the boy's voice calmed both mares. In some odd way, the strangeness of his clothes helped too. They were different than the humans either mare had seen before. The boy's black pants and a blue shirt somehow soothed them. *Nellie is too far into her birthing now to pay attention to the children*, Sadie thought.

Noah sat close to Nellie, wiping her down with a cloth, his gentle hands helped to soothe her.

A tall gaunt man in black pants, blue shirt, wearing a black hat came toward them, followed by the little girl named Rebecca. *What is he carrying?* Sadie thought. *Oh, I see, it's only a pail of water and a tube of some kind.*

He knelt next to Nellie and handed Noah a pair of gloves and a clean cloth. "Good job girl, you are doing well. The front legs are already out, soon the head will be too. You look like you've had a rough time beautiful."

Feeling as if Nellie was in good hands Sadie, stood quietly eyeing the little girl. I've never seen anyone dress like they do, except when they are going off to town. This is different. I believe they always dress this way, she thought, looking at the long dress on the little girl. As she walked over to her, Sadie lowered her head, her heart beating quite fast. Please don't let them turn us over to the auction.

Softly, Rebecca began petting Sadie. "You are so beautiful; you look like a horse angel all white like you are."

No one had ever said I was beautiful before or petted me so softly — not even Samuel, Sadie thought, sighing with delight. Perhaps these are some of the kind humans I heard talk of? Every bone in her body relaxed, and if she could purr, she would.

"It's a boy, a beautiful boy, Noah."

"Is it all over now Papa?"

"Not yet, she must pass the placenta, and we must hope that it all comes out too."

"You're doing great girl." He said softly, still wiping her down with a fresh cloth.

"Can we keep them, Papa?" Rebecca asked.

"That's something we will have to talk about. But I think it might be possible. The mares are both older, I think past breeding, but possibly they can learn to pull a cart."

"Papa, this angel still has milk. I think she gave birth not too long ago."

"Do you think she'd nurse Mary's foal? I mean if she'd take to it. After all, Mary died giving birth to it, just last night, and the goat's milk we are feeding it...."

"That is great thinking, Rebecca. It would be a good job for the mare. We all need jobs; it makes us all feel important." He answered looking at Sadie. "She is a beauty; what would you name her?"

"I'd call her Angel, Papa."

"Well, that's not a normal name for a mare, but I suspect the elders wouldn't mind this once. Angel it is."

I'm to be called Angel. Sadie thought. I like that name; it somehow sounds special. It looks like Nellie has passed the placenta. Perhaps all the walking helped ease the birthing.

"Nellie, he's beautiful and strong. Look, he's already trying to stand."

"Are we safe with these humans Sadie?"

"Yes, I think we are. They gave me a new name Nellie. They are going to call me Angel."

"Sadie, that's a lovely name.' Nellie said as she was getting to her feet. 'My little one is hungry, Sadie."

"Noah, take Rebecca and go on back to the barn, please. Tell your mother what has happened and get three lead ropes. I'll be here for much of the night before the foal is ready to walk the distance to the barn."

"Okay, Papa. Where do you think they came from? We don't have to give them, back do we?" Noah asked.

"I heard tell when I was in town yesterday, that there was a stampede at the auction three days ago, and the nurse mares that were scheduled for the slaughter house got away. I won't give these mares back to that fate. But perhaps, I'll send a bit of money to the auction house, so no one can complain we stole these mares."

Noah, and Rebecca both ran over to their father, and hugged him, before running off to the house.

"Did you hear that Nellie? We are safe. I believe we have a forever home."

Nellie looked up from watching her foal eat and smiled.

You can find Marta Moran Bishop at www.martamoranbishop.com and for all the latest news on events, authors, and new releases sign up for her newsletter.

Now for a short excerpt from her award-winning Dinky: The Nurse Mare's Foal

O_{ne}

Space

> Follow all your memories
> They will help you understand
> Space is a requirement
> To show respect for others

I don't want to remember when I first heard the term nurse mare's foal or who called me Dinky first. I had another name once, but only for a short time. I don't like to think about those times. When I do, I become frightened and angry. I would be so much happier today if I just could enjoy the moment as Chrome and Connella are doing. Unfortunately for me, I'm not in the mood to nap. Today I'm terrified of sleep for fear the dreams will come back. It's much better standing here in the middle of the field, letting the cool, gentle breeze flow through my mane, and feeling the warm sun on my back.

My black coat is beginning to turn white like Chrome's, and I know my tail looks beautiful with its multi-layers of colors swishing in the breeze. It is changing colors in layers from the bottom up. Soon it will be entirely gold, just as Chrome's tail is.

I love to stand and watch the ever-changing forest behind our field. Winter is still upon us, the trees are bare of leaves, and the snow is gone from the ground. Spring will be here soon. The days are growing longer giving us more time to play. Soon Marta and Ken will be spending more time outside, either with us or sitting at the table talking and watching us play.

Sometimes they will come and play with us, and at other times we will go over to the fence, watch them, and listen to their conversation. Connella said this year my lessons won't be baby lessons but ones for an adult horse. When I asked her what she meant by that, she just told me to wait and see. I hate it when others drop hints about things that will happen and then make me wait. I don't like waiting.

Today didn't start off well. Marta became annoyed with me quite early. Usually she's exceptionally polite about everything; she's even patient with Connella when she takes her time about going into her room for breakfast. It's Connella's way to make us all wait a bit. She pretends to ignore everyone as she looks at this and that, stops to smell a piece of rock, a pile of manure, or looks over the fence at the road or the forest beyond us. Whatever she can do to manipulate us all into waiting, she will do it. She especially likes to prove to me that she's next in line after Chrome. Often, she puts her ears back and chases me away if I try to go before her or if I stand too close to her.

It seems that every day someone tells me it's time for me to learn something new. Why can't they be clearer? Why is it so hard for me to grasp some of the things Chrome and Connella find so easy to understand? At mealtimes, even if Chrome and I stand at the fence waiting when it's time to go into our rooms, Connella makes sure she puts me in my place. Then it's Chrome with Connella standing behind him, and I don't quite know what to do. Am I supposed to go behind Connella? If this is the case, why must it be this way? Both of them have told me it's about learning my place in the herd. In the field, we all eat our hay together; there's plenty of food for everyone, so no one gets pushed aside. What is it about going into the barn for our grain that's different?

This morning began the same, except my new halter had a loose flap. Marta came over to fix it. She scolded Connella earlier for riling me up, which usually meant that I had to stay out of her way until she was willing to talk to me. Connella gets extremely annoyed if I get any attention, unless she has hers first.

It's odd, because if it's time for a cookie, Connella usually hangs back behind Chrome and me until Marta calls her. If Marta says, "Connella, get with your family," Connella will come up and stand with us, but if she says "Connella come on. Its cookie time," she goes into her room and waits, hanging her head out the window to get her cookie. It's fitting that her room is so close to the gate or Marta wouldn't be able to reach her.

Yet when it comes to meals, it changes; I'm unsure what makes meals different. I've tried talking to Connella and Chrome about it. They both say the same thing, "That's the way of things. You'll learn."

Well, back to what happened that caused today to be different. As I said, the flap on my halter was loose. Marta stood on my left fixing it, when Connella put her ears back and came toward me. I jumped toward Marta, and she fell. It was then that the day went from bad to worse.

After breakfast I tried to help Marta clean the stalls, but she didn't like it; she got annoyed with me and shut me in one of the stalls. Today instead of talking to me, she decided to lecture me while she cleaned the stalls. "Dinky, today you must learn about space. It's a part of learning respect for others," she said to me as I stood locked in my room waiting to be let out. "We all love you, even Connella, who it appears is the only one you always listen to. She forces you to understand and show her respect when she wants space. When you crowd others when they don't want it, and you get too close to them, you're disrespecting them." As she finished cleaning Chrome's stall she continued. (I wanted to go out in the field, but I knew she wouldn't let me until she was finished.)

"Dinky, until you learn to listen to me and not tip over the wheelbarrow full of manure, you must stay in your room." So, I was stuck, a captive audience, as she continued to lecture me. "It can also become risky if you do it when Ken or I are walking you on the lead rope or you jump toward me as you did earlier. We're going to begin your lessons immediately. Both yesterday and today could have been extremely dangerous, Dinky."

I didn't like the sound of any of this and was getting really antsy to go out and finish my breakfast. Still, she went on, "Chrome and Connella took their halters easily. On the other hand, you thought you knew what was coming and didn't wait for your halter. It's not acceptable for you to push through everybody the way you did last night. I don't care if you think I'm going to let you all into the round pen and allow you all to run and jump with no one in control. It's about time you learned differently. You're a big boy now and it's time you learn some manners. If you don't, someday someone will get hurt. It might be Ken, Chrome, Connella, me, or you. So today we will begin the first of many lessons. You'll learn appropriate behavior about space. I will not have you be a threat to yourself or others."

I stood there looking at her with my cutest little boy expression, but it was of no help. Today it didn't matter how sweet I appeared. There would be no stopping her.

Still feeling ashamed of myself after being chastised in front of everyone, the lessons began. She made me stand away from her; if I tried to come near her before she called me, she pushed me away. Then we had the move over exercises. Sometimes I only had to move my hind quarters and sometimes all of me. Until she decided when, I couldn't come close or cuddle. The big "NO" apparently is if I try to push at her or go first. It was awful, especially when she said, "Dinky, we'll do this lesson a lot over the coming weeks." After she left, Chrome nipped me when I tried to get him to play. "I'm not in the mood right now. Dinky, give me some space."

Still, I persisted. I had to have some answers, and so before Chrome went to take his nap, I asked him, "Chrome, why is it so hard for me to learn these things?"

He said, "I think it's because you didn't have other horses around you or a mom to teach you these things when you were young, Dinky. If you had the proper weaning it wouldn't be so hard. When I grew up, my mother began my weaning by pushing me away."

"What's weaning, Chrome?"

"It's when the time comes for you to eat adult food and not drink your mother's milk anymore."

"I stopped drinking my mother's milk months ago, Chrome. Was that weaning?" I asked.

"Not really, Dinky. It was much too early for you to leave your mom. You should have spent about six months with her, and then you would have been moved in with the other foals but kept close enough to your mother. Your mother and other adult horses should still have been near enough to protect and teach you. It's a long process—one you didn't learn, my friend. It's what teaches you about space."

"Chrome, if I never had those things you're describing, how will I learn it all now? I don't like being confused half the time. And I don't like being scolded, though sometimes it's fun to get Connella riled up," I replied.

"I'm not quite sure, Dinky. I know you don't like to think about the past, but I think you might have to. Even when you first came here, you didn't talk about it, not even when Connella and I asked you questions. I honestly believe you'll have to think about those times if you're going to move forward. And you should talk about them too."

"You don't understand, Chrome. It's so scary to remember, and I feel so terrified—almost as if the darkness will kill me."

"Still, I think you must face your fears, Dinky. Then you'll be able to understand things easier."

I didn't like the tone the conversation was taking, so I walked off thinking. Maybe space meant I could only get close to someone when I was invited. I didn't like that either. Why should I have to be the one to lose out on what I needed? Chrome told me that it was only a matter of time, and then I'd feel happy about my place. I would have to earn it. Lessons were hard work, and I wasn't quite sure I liked them.

I was still unsure what the difference was between a lesson and play. But I did know that the lessons about space weren't my favorite. In fact, I was sure I didn't like them at all. They reminded me of some of the bad times. Oh, I didn't want to think about the bad times. I hated to ruminate on those dark, scary, lonely times. I was afraid. I knew today the memories would come, what with Chrome and Connella napping and me standing here thinking about today's lesson and what it all meant.

Don't get me wrong, most days here were terrific. I felt loved and wanted. Sometimes the memories were wonderful ones, and I laughed and felt happy. Then there were days like today when I got reprimanded. It was then that I started recalling things and the darkness came alive. Usually, I could find something to distract me or a game to play. I was afraid today I might not be as successful. The lesson on space made me feel alone, small, and helpless again. As the memories washed over me, I felt myself going down a long black tunnel. The sunlight had vanished. The familiar forest behind our field was gone. I was alone in my mind in the dark again.

www.ingramcontent.com/pod-product-compliance
Lightning Source LLC
Chambersburg PA
CBHW072031170626
46811CB00008B/3027